SEAGULL & SEA DRAGON

For my family
—S. G.

ALADDIN | An imprint of Simon & Schuster Children's Publishing Division | 1230 Avenue of the Americas, New York, New York 10020 First Aladdin hardcover edition June 2019 | Copyright © 2019 by Sydni Gregg | All rights reserved, including the right of reproduction in whole or in part in any form. | ALADDIN and related logo are registered trademarks of Simon & Schuster, Inc. | For information about special discounts for bulk purchases, please contact Simon & Schuster Special Sales at 1-866-506-1949 or business@simonandschuster.com. | The Simon & Schuster Speakers Bureau can bring authors to your live event. For more information or to book an event contact the Simon & Schuster Speakers Bureau at 1-866-248-3049 or visit our website at www.simonspeakers.com. | Designed by Tiara Iandiorio | The illustrations for this book were rendered digitally. | The text of this book was set in Hank BT, Blend, and Gothic 821. | Manufactured in China 0419 SCP | 2 3 4 5 6 7 8 9 10 Library of Congress Cataloging-in-Publication Data | Names: Gregg, Sydni, author, illustrator. | Title: Seagull and Sea Dragon / written and illustrated by Sydni Gregg. | Description: First Aladdin hardcover edition. | New York : Aladdin, 2019. | Summary: A seagull flies through the sky and a sea dragon swims in the ocean, each wondering about the other's home until they meet and discover their worlds are more similar than they imagined. | Identifiers: LCCN 2018023278 (print) | LCCN 2018029098 (eBook) ISBN 9781534420496 (eBook) | ISBN 9781534420489 (hardcover) | Subjects: | CYAC: Gulls—Fiction. | Seadragons—Fiction. Sky—Fiction. | Seas—Fiction. | Classification: LCC PZ7.1.G7412 (eBook) | LCC PZ7.1.G7412 Se 2019 (print) | DDC [E]—dc23 LC record available at https://lccn.loc.gov/2018023278

SEAGULL &
SEA DRAGON

SYDNI GREGG

ALADDIN
New York London Toronto Sydney New Delhi

I am a seagull.

Every day I fly high in the sky.
And every day I wonder:

What's it like down beneath the water?

Some things seem
a little familiar.

"Are those sea trees?"

"Do all sea trees have beaks?"

Some things are mysterious.

I am a sea dragon.

Every day I swim deep in the sea.
And every day I wonder:

What's it like up there in the sky?

Some things seem so different.

"Is that a school of sky fish?"

"Their fins are so big!"

Some things are a bit magical.

I have so many questions.
And there's so
much I don't know.

"Look! Are those
giant bubbles?"

"Why would they be floating
out of the water?"

Sometimes it makes me feel . . .
SCARED.

"You're a sea tree!"

"I'm a seagull."

"I'm a sea dragon."

"I'm not a sea tree ...
but there is something
like it. Coral!"

"I'm not a sky fish! But seagulls
travel together like fish do.
We're called a flock!"

"Those lights you see
are really moon jellyfish!
They are beautiful."

"And those giant
bubbles are hot-air balloons!
Sometimes I even see humans
riding in them."

"Wait. What?"

"These are feathers! They are kind of like scales, but they help us fly!"

"These aren't leaves! They are fins. They are kind of like wings, and they help us swim."

"I'd love to hear more about the sky!"

"And I'd love to hear more about the sea!"

"I'm *so* glad I got to talk to you!"

"I can't wait to learn more! But there is one more thing I want to say."